Bunny and Me

Story and Photographs by Adele Aron Greenspun
Photographic Enhancement by Joanie Schwarz

Cartwheel
·B·O·O·K·S·®

SCHOLASTIC INC.

New York Toronto London Auckland Sydney Mexico City New Delhi Hong Kong

No part of this publication may be reproduced, or stored in a retrieval system, or transmitted in any form or by any means, electronic, mechanical, photocopying, recording, or otherwise, without written permission of the publisher. For information regarding permissions, write to Scholastic Inc., Attention: Permissions Department, 555 Broadway, New York, NY 10012.

ISBN 439-14700-X

Copyright © 2000 by Adele Aron Greenspun.
All rights reserved. Published by Scholastic Inc.
SCHOLASTIC, CARTWHEEL BOOKS and associated logos
are trademarks and/or registered trademarks of Scholastic Inc.

Library of Congress Cataloging-in-Publication Data available.

10 9 8 7 6 5 4 3 2 1   0/0 01 02 03 04
Printed in Singapore   46
First printing, March 2000

To Erica, Joanie, Ariel, and Frances—A.A.G.

Baby sees Bunny.

Bunny sees Baby.

Baby touches Bunny's nose.

Bunny touches Baby's toes.

Baby pops bubbles.

Bunny pops bubbles.

Bunny wears beads.

Baby wears beads.

Bunny kisses Baby's doll.

Baby laughs.

Baby opens a book. Bunny wants to look.

Baby chases Bunny.

Bunny chases a ball.

Bunny hops away.

"Come back, Bunny!"

"Where are you?"

Is Bunny behind the tree?

Is Bunny in the bushes?

Is Bunny under the bench?

Is Bunny inside the basket?

"There's Bunny!"

"Bunny is in the basket!"

Funny buddies.

Baby and Bunny.